To Lois, who always reminded us that we would
CATCH A COLD if we went outside without a jacket.

And to Mike who would nod his head in agreement
as he stood there wearing shorts and a t-shirt.

Your love and laughter will forever
bring a smile to our faces and inspire us.

MiLo Ink Books
www.miloinkbooks.com

How to Catch a Cold / by Adam T. Newman; illustrations by Susan G. Young
Text copyright ©2012 by MiLo INK Books / Adam T. Newman
Illustrations copyright ©2012 by Susan G. Young

ISBN-13: 978-0615706870
ISBN-10: 0615706878

First edition

HOW to CatCh a Cold

written by Adam T. Newman

illustrated by Susan G. Young

The school bell rings.
I run to my chair.

I turn to my friend Brian,
but he isn't there!

Maybe as he walked to school
he fell into a hole,
where he's being held captive
by an angry, old mole.

THAT WAS MONDAY

On Tuesday, when the school bell rang
I hurried to my seat.

I noticed Brian was still missing,
and now, so was Pete!

What could have happened?
This is very, very odd.

Was Pete fished out of bed
by a boy-fishing cod?

"Ms. Rose! Ms. Rose! Ms. Rose!" I cry.
"My friends are all missing
and I don't know why.

They're not at school, and I'm concerned.
Have you called the police?
What have you learned?"

With a sweet, calming voice
Ms. Rose smiled and said,
"No one is being held captive
or was fished out of bed.

I spoke to their parents,
and I was told,
our friends are not missing,
they just caught a cold."

"THEY CAUGHT A COLD?"

Where do COLDS live?
Where do they hide?

Do they dwell inside cookie jars
or on top of trash cans outside?

After school I ran home,
didn't even stop for a snack.

I just finished my homework
and prepared my attack.

To catch a butterfly, you use a net.
To catch a baseball, you wear a mitt.
I'll pack an umbrella
in case COLDS like to spit.

I'll take three jars of honey,
and twenty rolls of clear tape.
I'll strap lint rollers to my hips
and wear a flypaper cape.

"LET'S GO CATCH A COLD!"

I went outside to catch a COLD.
I searched up in a tree.

I saw something moving on a leaf,
but it was just a buzzing bee.

I held out my baseball mitt
and looked up in the sky,
just as a bird flew overhead
and pooped in my eye.

"They say that's good luck!"

I moved my search inside my house.
I looked behind the drapes.
I said, really bold, "I caught you, COLD!"
But it was only a few old grapes.

"Or maybe they're raisins."

In case COLDS were invisible
I splattered honey in the air.

I even used my lint rollers
to search through my dog's hair.

But no COLDS were found there.

"I hope you're not catching a cold,"
Mommy looked at me and said.

How'd she know what I was doing?
Was it written on my head?

"BY DOZE IS TUFFY," I told her.
My words all sounded funny.

I called my Mom, "BOM,"
And my nose was very runny.

What was going on with me?
I seemed to have some issues.

Forget trying to catch a COLD,
I'd rather find some tissues!

I plopped my head upon my bed.
I was so tired and beat.

"I guess I'm not catching a COLD today."
And I accepted my defeat.

"Goodnight COLD, wherever you are."

I woke up the next morning
with a billion boogers galore.

My nose was super stuffy,
and my throat was really sore.

I had a raspy voice
which made me sound old.

You're staying home from school," Mom said.
"You caught a COLD.".

"I caught a COLD? Whoo hoo!
Now if I could only remember where I put it."

About the Author

Adam T. Newman's childhood consisted of sports, reading comic books and playing with action figures. His love for film, writing and cartoons led him cross country to Los Angeles where he landed a job working for a children's animation company.

Adam has worked for numerous studios as an Art Director and Graphic Designer.

He is also the recipient of the prestigious "World's Greatest Dad" award which was presented by his two wonderful kids in the form of a t-shirt.

About the Illustrator

Susan G. Young was born in Baton Rouge, LA to a large family full of over-educated engineers, doctors and world leaders. Being the youngest in the family, and having no other means by which to cause her parents anxiety, Susan left her stable job to pursue a career in the Arts.

Susan acquired her MFA in Illustration from Savannah College of Art and Design. She currently works from her home in Brooklyn as a freelance illustrator and is also a professor at Pratt Institute.

Made in the USA
Lexington, KY
07 December 2012